Two Mice in a Boat

Story adapted by Katharine Holabird
from the TV episode

Based on the classic picture books
by Katharine Holabird and Helen Craig

Grosset & Dunlap

GROSSET & DUNLAP
Published by the Penguin Group
Penguin Group (USA) Inc., 375 Hudson Street, New York,   .0014, U.S.A.
Penguin Group (Canada), 90 Eglinton Avenue East, Suite 700, Toronto, Ontario,
Canada M4P 2Y3 (a division of Pearson Penguin Canada Inc.)
Penguin Books Ltd, 80 Strand, London WC2R 0RL, England
Penguin Ireland, 25 St Stephen's Green, Dublin 2, Irela~
(a division of Penguin Books Ltd)
Penguin Group (Australia), 250 Camberwell Road, Camber..., ..toria 3124,
Australia (a division of Pearson Australia Group Pty Ltd)
Penguin Books India Pvt Ltd, 11 Community Centre,
Panchsheel Park, New Delhi - 110 017, India
Penguin Group (NZ), Cnr Airborne and Rosedale Roads, Albany, Auckland 1310,
New Zealand (a division of Pearson New Zealand Ltd)
Penguin Books (South Africa) (Pty) Ltd, 24 Sturdee Avenue, Rosebank,
Johannesburg 2196, South Africa

Penguin Books Ltd, Registered Offices:
80 Strand, London WC2R 0RL, England

Angelina Ballerina™ © 2006 Helen Craig Ltd. and Katharine Holabird. The Angelina
Ballerina name and character and the dancing Angelina logo are trademarks of HIT
Entertainment Ltd., Katharine Holabird and Helen Craig. Reg. U.S. Pat. & Tm. Off. Used
under license by Penguin Young Readers Group. All rights reserved. Published by Grosset
& Dunlap, a division of Penguin Young Readers Group, 345 Hudson Street, New York, New
York 10014. GROSSET & DUNLAP is a trademark of Penguin Group (USA) Inc.
Manufactured in China.

Special markets ISBN 0-670-06116-6   10 9 8 7 6 5 4 3 2

It was bedtime, but Angelina wasn't tired. She'd found her father's old Miller's Pond Boat Carnival trophy.

"Oh, Dad! I'm determined to win this year," she said.

"And how are you going to decorate your boat, Angelina?" asked her father.

"Well," began Angelina, "it will be a huge white swan, with gold thrones for Alice and me, the Swan Princesses!"

"It sounds lovely, dear, but don't count on being teamed up with Alice," warned Mrs. Mouseling gently.

The next day at school, Miss Chalk announced the boat-decorating teams. "Priscilla with Penelope, Flora with William, Angelina with Sammy . . ."

"Sammy!" said Angelina, shocked.

"Angelina!" sputtered Sammy.

"Alice with Henry," continued Miss Chalk. Alice looked horrified.

"It's all about teamwork!" said Miss Chalk over the din of unhappy mice.

Angelina and Sammy lined up to collect their boat from Captain Miller.

"I wouldn't be seen dead in a sissy swan boat," muttered Sammy.

"Well, you wouldn't catch me on some stupid pirate ship!" spat Angelina. She sighed as she looked at Sammy's plans. "We're never going to agree, so we'll just have to try and . . ."

"Work together," they both muttered.

The next day, they drew a line down the middle of the boat. They decided to decorate one-half each. "Don't go over the line," warned Angelina sternly.

"Don't worry, I won't!" said Sammy.

Down near the river, Alice and Henry were decorating their boat with sweets.

"One for the boat, one for you!" they said happily, popping candies into each other's mouths.

On the day of the carnival, Angelina and Sammy
got ready early and went to try out their boat on the
river.

"It floats!" cried Angelina when they eventually
managed to launch it.

The two mice turned around when they heard a rumbling noise behind them. It was the builder mouse, Mr. Ratchett.

"Nice boat you've got there!" he said. "What's she called?"

"The Swan Princess," said Angelina.

"The Pirate King!" shouted Sammy.

"That's a big name for a small boat!" chuckled Mr. Ratchett as he carried on up the road.

The mouselings jumped on board.

"I think we're sinking," said Sammy as he watched water seeping into the boat.

"I said that cannon was too heavy!" cried Swan Princess Angelina furiously.

"It's probably that stupid bird's head," muttered Pirate Sammy.

They began to throw things out of the boat as fast as they could, until there was absolutely nothing left.

"We're floating now!" said Sammy.

"Downstream!" shouted Angelina desperately.
"Where are the oars?"

"Over there!" cried Sammy, pointing to the oars
floating away in the water.

Meanwhile, Alice and Henry had nearly finished
their boat, but they'd spent quite a lot of time
eating the decorations and felt a little sick!

Farther downstream, Angelina and Sammy were moving fast!

"We've got to stop!" yelled Angelina.

"I can see a tree stump up ahead!" bellowed Sammy.

"We need some rope to loop over it. Look!" Angelina had seen something.

"Vines!" they both said together.

As the little boat sped along, the two frightened mice grabbed onto the vines.

"Hold on!" shouted Sammy.

The vines broke away from the bank, and Angelina found the longest one. Angelina and Sammy both grabbed onto it just as the boat reached the tree stump.

They struggled to loop the vine over the stump
and pulled themselves onto the bank.

"We have to get back to Miller's Pond!" cried a
desperate Angelina.

Just then, Sammy and Angelina heard a *chug chug*
behind them.

"Mr. Ratchett!" they both shouted, relieved.

At Miller's Pond, the carnival was under way.
Alice and Henry were dressed as candy canes,
and their boat was decorated entirely with candy
wrappers!

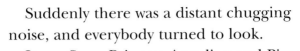

Suddenly there was a distant chugging
noise, and everybody turned to look.

It was Swan Princess Angelina and Pirate
Sammy. They were floating along in the sky on
the end of Mr. Ratchett's crane!

Everyone at Miller's Pond clapped and
cheered as Angelina and Sammy were slowly
lowered toward the water.

SPLASH! They landed a bit too close to Priscilla
and Penelope Pinkpaws' boat. It was decorated as
a huge pink ballet shoe. "Our lovely shoe!" they
squeaked. "Now it's soaking wet!"

Angelina and Sammy giggled together.

"The winners of the boat-decorating contest are
Alice and Henry," said Captain Miller a little later.
"But this year's prize for teamwork goes to Angelina
and Sammy!"

Mr. Mouseling introduced Angelina to his old boating partner—Sammy's dad! "We never won a teamwork prize," said Mr. Watts. "We were always arguing."

"No we weren't!" replied Mr. Mouseling.

Angelina and Sammy giggled.

"YOU keep the trophy," said Angelina.

"No, you keep it," replied Sammy.

The two mouselings, and their fathers, carried on arguing and laughing until the sun went down and it was time for every tired mouse to go home to bed.